I0618435

THE UNJUST, DUST, AND HOPE

ROB VAGLE

DOG COPILOT PRESS

The Unjust, Dust, And Hope

Copyright © 2025 by Rob Vagle

Published by Dog Copilot Press

Cover art "Ominous glowing crystal ball background" © by Robert Spriggs/Dreamstime.com

Cover art "Wild West Town" © by YaroslavGerzhedovich/iStockphoto.com

Book and Cover design Copyright © 2025 Dog Copilot Press

ISBN-13: 978-0615825335

ISBN-10: 0615825338

CONTENTS

THE UNJUST, DUST, AND HOPE

L eroy Roosevelt's corpse started growing even before they cut him down from the tree they hanged him from, his neck swelling around the rope, his feet ballooning within his boots—the very boots his friend, Cleve Biddle, had given him.

He had been hanged for one reason: he was a black man who spoke to a white woman in the center of town. Schoolteacher Mary Wilson inquired about his days shackled by slavery and his life after the Civil War as a free man.

When the Johnson brothers confronted Leroy about talking to her, Leroy replied, "Nobody tells me what do anymore. The Emancipation Proclamation ensures I'm no longer a slave."

Mary Wilson insisted she had engaged the conversation and not Leroy. The brothers ignored her claim and gathered up a lynch mob and fired up the lie Leroy had attempted to rape her. When Mary Wilson protested, they brushed her off as distressed and confused.

The hanging happened quickly, Leroy's guilt and fate instantly decided by the mob without debate.

Deputy Sheriff Cletus Thomas, the only man present with a badge, never spoke out against the hanging and even provided the rope.

Leroy hanged from the tree until his people caught word. Family and friends ventured out in the evening to gather him up.

Sabina, Leroy's wife, threw herself on top of him in the back of the wagon. She wailed and thrashed, her hands grabbing at him, fingers working to grip his shirt, which was now tight around his shoulders and suspenders taut. Her mind was engulfed by grief, but some part of her realized something wasn't right about his clothes. That realization would come into focus later.

Leroy was placed in a simple pine board box and lowered into a grave. Before the first shovel of dirt was thrown back into the hole, his feet were bare and free of the leather boots.

As if the fresh grave fed his corpse, he grew rapidly, much quicker than a weed. His feet pressed up against the end of the box, splitting wood. Hours after his burial, he surfaced, his burgeoning corpse pushing dirt into a ridge-line piling around him.

By the time the sun came up his body had grown across the cemetery, disrupting graves and over-turning wooden crosses. He was naked, his dark skin dusty with dirt. His feet struck the wall of the church next to the cemetery, his heels caving in the wooden foundation. The stench of decomposing flesh permeated the air and attracted the whole town's attention.

Anyone who pushed at the body was pushed back harder by the growing corpse, and the corpse threatened to mow right over them. Men tied rope around his toes and pulled with horses to drag the corpse away, but the corpse grew even as the horses pulled.

The men who hanged Leroy were the most astonished. They watched the corpse move across the leveled church, the head and heels plowing up the earth.

The Johnson brothers attempted to rig dynamite in the path of the extending legs (each foot taller than a horse) but they were buried by the plowed dirt of the corpse's heels. In an attempt to save the Johnsons, Deputy Thomas swung an ax at the left foot, each blow glancing off as if striking black granite. He swung again and again until he slipped under the plowed earth and was smothered by dirt.

The blooming corpse knocked down houses and buildings on every side of it, the town filled with the sound of splintering wood, collapsing roofs, and shattering glass.

An earth shuddering rumble overwhelmed the town of Dobson that day. Most citizens believed Armageddon had come in the form of a black man's corpse. People prayed to the sky, some prayed to Leroy himself, but no words could stop the corpse.

Citizens fled the town. Sabina rode in the back of a wagon stocked full of what belongings her family could save. She couldn't turn away from the tragedy of her husband's death, and the horror still growing. Her hands rested on her stomach and she thought about her child growing there and the father it now would not have. Their first child. Leroy was lynched out of hatred and ignorance. She was angry enough to say let it be—let his corpse grow for the injustice. Yet this scared her and left her restless. She had to ask herself: when would it end? When would her husband be at peace?

Pray that the good lord knew when to stop Leroy Roosevelt's corpse.

TO UNDERSTAND what happened out in the desert—in what had been the town of Dobson in the Arizona Territory—on February 5th, 1877, you'll need to know what had come before. Whenever I wonder where to begin, my head hurts. I could go back a decade to the Emancipation Proclamation. I could go as far back as when African slaves were brought to the shores of America. When to begin? It's all important.

My history: in 1855 I became a freed slave. From the South and my master I fled, away from the supremacy over blacks, to the North where most believed the slave should be free but thought the Negro inferior, in intellect and temperament. Then to the West where territories such as Oregon were legislating to keep coloreds out. The constitution proclaimed we were equal, but we were merely separate. We were the "other" evident in the behaviors and attitudes of many whites.

All of these things are important to the story I'm

telling you. These things were ingredients that created Leroy's death and the aftermath.

I guess the best place to start would be the recent present: August 18th, 1875. That was the day the prognosticators came into play. Leroy's life, let alone my own, would never be the same.

We lived in a town called White Rock, just a hundred miles south of Dobson. I worked as a boot-black on the front porch of the Hotel Beaumont, polishing boots of traveling salesmen, businessmen, and entrepreneurs.

On August the eighteenth, the heat baked the air, permeating the shade underneath the porch of where I stood at the railing and stared at the board-walk across the street. My shirt stuck to the sweat on my back and I wiped my brow with the handkerchief from my back pocket. My hands were stiffening up and had seen nimbler, spry days. My knees ached. My back, too. The sun gleamed off everything: the windows of the shops, the metal of passing stages and wagons, their wheels creaking and turning as lackadaisically as a horse's tail flicking at the flies on its hide. Dust rose in the air from tromping horses and rolling wagons and underneath feet of men and women venturing out in the high heat of day. There was a tumultuous sea of hats out there above white faces, and umbrellas of various colors to shade ladies' faces.

Out of this multitude came Leroy Roosevelt, a colored man over six feet tall and built like an ox.

I had raised Leroy as my own. He was tied face down on the back of a trail boss's horse when I first saw him eight years earlier. This boss had rode into White Rock's colored community and dumped Leroy on us. He said he didn't have a place for a colored boy who couldn't hold his tongue and he left town as quickly as he came. At that time, the Washingtons and I were the only coloreds in town, besides Otis. The Washingtons already had a large family. Eight children. Six boys and two girls. I had no family, had nobody but myself to fend for. The Washingtons had enough mouths to feed and bodies to clothe. Although I was old enough to be Leroy's grandfather, I took him in. He was an older boy on the cusp of being a man and I saw Leroy had a need. He needed a disciplined, steady hand. He had yet to learn to read and write. Leroy had skill with horses and blacksmithing, but he needed an education. That more than anything would set him free.

But on that August the eighteenth, I smiled at his

approach and replaced the handkerchief in my back pocket. My visits with him would be less in the coming days because he was engaged to his sweet Sabina who lived in Dobson. He'd be moving in a week and it gladdened my heart for the unexpected sight of him that day.

"What in God's great world brings you here, Leroy?" I asked.

He leaped the front steps with a piece of paper in his hand and joined me in the shade of the porch.

"Lady McMasters sent me a note," Leroy said. "She says she has a message for me."

She was a prognosticator from New Orleans who helped businessmen with investments and business deals. She came to White Rock once a year because the entrepreneurs in the West paid her to come. Obviously, they got something out her services because they kept asking her back. What she actually gave them, I'd like to know, because I never believed anyone who claimed to see the future.

"What business does she have to do with you?" I asked.

He looked down at me with a pained expression, his eyes wide with worry—my first indication the visit wasn't a pleasant one. "I've never spoken to her before," he said. "Yet her note says it's of great importance that I meet with her."

Like a dazed man he walked past me and into the hotel, leaving me blinking the dripping sweat from my eyes.

Through the open front door I saw Leroy meet with Lady McMasters in the lobby. No colored man would be allowed upstairs even though there were no signs stating so. She talked to him as she waved a fan in front of her face. At the front desk, Bobby laughed at something she said.

Then Leroy came out the Hotel Beaumont holding his head as if it might fall off his shoulders. He was hunched over, his whole body shuddering. I found it disheartening that this emotion possessed him. It had transformed him into a child.

I grabbed his arm. "Get a hold of yourself."

We were alone on the front porch of the hotel and for that I was grateful. Main Street was busy—wagons creaked as they rolled by, horses hooves pounding the hard packed earth, dogs barking from outside the saloon down the street. I never knew when someone might come out of the hotel for a polish and I sure didn't want someone, especially a white, see the messy state Leroy was in.

"Cleve," he said, "that fortune teller reminded me of something terrible."

"What's that?" I led him to my first of three chairs lined up along the wall to the right of the front door.

He sat down hard and grunted when he settled.

Dust devils blew by in the street, laying a fine layer of dust onto the porch. A bootblack's job is never done in this dusty desert. When the dust wasn't in my nose, the air smelled like manure.

"My death and the mess it will cause," Leroy said.

"Have you been taking sips from a flask?" I asked.

Leroy shook his head. I had expected him to be angry by the insult. Leroy wasn't the type to dance with a bottle.

"Son, why are you acting this way. A fortune teller is more full of lies than truth. Why you believing this white woman for?"

"She's not the only one who told me," he said.

"Somebody else gave you the same fortune?"

"That's right."

"You care to elaborate?"

"There was this old woman who lived on the same plantation as me back in Alabama when we were still slaves. She practiced voodoo and her home was filled with candles and roots and all sorts of smelly things. She helped her neighbors by curing whatever ailed them, mixing up powders and potions and the like. She told fortunes, too. My grandma used to visit her all the time and hear about the future she wouldn't be alive to see."

"And what did this voodoo woman tell you?"

"Her name was Delilah and she told me my death would be the downfall of this nation." Leroy broke a moment and sighed. "I don't want to die, Cleve. According to two women gifted with the sight, my death will cause more death. A man's death should be private and small. Not Armageddon."

"Were there words identical? Start with voodoo lady. Now, what did she say? Exact words."

He quieted down and sat up straight and squared his shoulders. He looked up and thought a moment.

"She said that 'The ground will crack upon my death, as my corpse will weigh heavy on the land.'"

He looked at me then and blinked.

"Those words worried you, son? I didn't hear anything to be upset about."

"I was a young'n' then and didn't know what to think."

"What did Lady McMasters tell you today?"

His shoulders sagged and his eyes lowered to the

pine boards under our feet. "She said your death will be the death of this country. Your corpse will bury thousands of souls and split the land."

"There are similarities there, but it's all packed with vagueness and obfuscation."

"Ob-what, sir?"

I grabbed his shoulder and shook him. "There's no details, but there's enough message to get you worked up. Why, Leroy, there's not a single detail where you can pinpoint your death. There's no when or how or where or who. It's left up to your imagination, boy. And those prognosticators have your imagination working, running wild and untamed. It's all in your head, boy."

He swayed a little. "I hear you, I hear you. 'though my mind still has a dark cloud upon it."

"Don't let them inside your head anymore than they already are," I said. "Rein in your imagination. You have your future with Sabina to consider."

He nodded, not looking me in the eye and I thought he might just be placating me.

"Alright," he said, standing up. "I do have work to do. Sabina will be expecting me in little more than a week."

He walked through the dust clouds a little taller than when he had first come out of the Beaumont, but he wandered the street aimlessly for a moment before striking east towards home.

Like an omen (but I didn't know it then) Otis Turning's wagon passed the hotel. It was a black wagon with tall walls. On the three sides large, blazing red letters: Tonics, ointments, trinkets, and charms.

White rock had such a small colored population that it was impossible not to know of Otis, one colored man who kept to himself on his property outside of town. What we did know, colored and white folk alike, is that he was a traveling merchant who covered White Rock and neighboring communities, and twice a year made trips to St. Louis to restock his goods. He paid colored boys to do chores around his homestead and run errands. Otis also did business from his home performing parlor sessions where he would talk to the dead, reveal futures, and give advice to people who paid for it. It was snake oil to me. He played on the fears and ignorance of people.

As Leroy vanished behind Otis's wagon, an inexplicable feeling of loss washed over me. Puzzled, I leaned on the railing, my head poking out from underneath the porch so that sunlight baked across my face. What had I lost? I raised Leroy. He may have been on the cusp of becoming a man when I took him under my wing, but I taught him to read and write and do arithmetic.

I've never known him to believe in superstition and I've even warned him to keep away from Otis. Yet there Leroy went—twisted up inside and out over something a prognosticator said.

I guess, in that moment, I felt I had failed. I had failed to whip the gullibility from Leroy and instill a vibrant skepticism.

And my skepticism was as stubborn and merciless as the desert sun.

LADY MCMASTERS HAD some words for me the next day in front of a businessman staying at the hotel.

Mr. Chester hailed from Louisiana. Dressed in crisp white shirt, a velvet vest with a gold chained pocket watch. He wore a round hat, and had a neat and trimmed mustache. He had walked out on the porch with a newspaper, glanced at my empty chairs, but not at me, the old colored bootblack. Then he proceeded to walk to my first chair, sit down, prop his feet up and lift his newspaper in front of his face so he wouldn't have to look at me.

Mr. Chester was a frequent guest at the hotel—about four times a year. Every visit he got his boots polished. He would not look at me nor say a word. Simply put: I did my job, then I got paid.

I could tell where the businessmen and entrepreneurs came from by the way they treated me. The men from the South acted like Mr. Chester, ignoring me and sticking their noses up even as they pay for my services. The businessmen from the North on the other hand, they'd at least make eye contact with me and verbally request a polish. However, those northern businessmen wouldn't talk unless I prodded them. Poor conversationalists they were.

This is the way of things since the slaves were set free. Men explore and settle the frontier. Men travel. They bring their prejudices with them like luggage.

I hunkered down on my stool, snapped my cloth in the air, ready to first clean his boots, but that's when Lady McMasters made her appearance, stepping out of the hotel.

She strolled towards us, her wide skirt just gliding over the floor, her feet not making much more noise than a couple of fists knocking on wood. The handle of her open umbrella rested on one shoulder. The umbrella was turquoise and white with frilly edges that blurred as she turned the handle.

Her emerald green eyes were aimed right at me.

Mr. Chester lowered his newspaper enough to give the Lady a put upon look.

"Cleve Biddle," she said, her voice dripping with enough sweetness to attract bees. "Your friend Leroy needs your help. He cannot be afraid. He needs to carry on."

Mr. Chester said, "Pardon?"

She paid Mr. Chester no mind.

How did she know my name? Never had I exchanged a word with her before. Was Leroy in trouble?

Before I could find the words, she pivoted around and walked off the porch to the waiting coach in front. My heart stirred in worry.

"She gives fortunes for free to a colored, yet she charges me for her services." I looked at Mr. Chester and he pulled the newspaper up over his face again. "Well, boy," he said, "you get what you paid for, which is precisely nothing."

Red, red, angry red filled my head at Mr. Chester's words but I wouldn't let it surpass the concern I had for Leroy. I snapped my cloth three times, the anger slipping away. I held the jar of tallow to my nose and inhaled. The raw animal smell brought me back to the task at hand.

Truth was there were ways she could have found out my name—the front desk, for example. I'd have to wait until my workday was done before I checked on Leroy. The Lord would look after him until then.

Near dusk Owen Clark walked by the hotel carrying his lunch bucket on his way home from work at the saloon down the street. Owen was the youngest boy of the family that lived next door to Leroy.

I waved at him and said, "Have you seen Leroy today?"

He stopped in front of the steps of the hotel and waved at the dust setting in the air from a passing stage. "No, I haven't seen him since yesterday. And yesterday he wasn't talking to nobody."

"Anybody," I said, correcting him.

"That's right," he replied, but I didn't think he realized his double negative.

An hour later it was dark and I was done working. I packed up my kit and walked to Leroy's. When I arrived there, lantern light flickered behind window. A full moon hung suspended above the roof. Smoke from Leroy's chimney climbed up the moon's face.

I opened the front gate and walked through. I stepped under his porch overhang and even I had to duck. Leroy was tall and I wondered how he dealt with coming in and out of his front door each day.

I knocked hard, pounding a half dozen times. Then I called out his name. "I'm coming in if you don't answer me," I said.

There was a scrape of a chair across the floor and the shuffling of feet, the floorboards creaking as he came to the door.

The door opened and Leroy stood there with no shirt and suspenders holding up his pants. He held the lantern in his hand and the light highlighted his solemn face and eyes droopy and red from lack of sleep.

"Something bothering you, son?" I asked.

"A cloud of oppression is on me, Cleve. Ever since yesterday with that woman from New Orleans," he said.

He stepped aside, opening the door wide and I walked in. There was a kettle in the fire. It smelled of stew. At last the man hadn't lost all good sense not to eat. I sat down at the table in a chair that creaked even under my slight weight. I thought it might break on me.

When I looked down underneath me, Leroy said,

"If that chair can hold me, it can hold little old you, so keep your words to yourself."

I grumbled and watched him hang the lantern on its peg and sat down across from me. He was never one to tolerate my criticisms.

"Leroy," I said, "when I was back in the South, I knew many ignorant slaves who believed that if they carried a particular root on their persons, this would prevent them from being beat by their masters. I never believed it. Did you?"

"No, sir," he said. His shoulders were hunched, his head hung over the table.

"When the promise of gold was hailed in California, the whites encouraged a rumor that the black man had an inner and natural ability to find gold, so blacks should be barred from entering California. An excuse to keep blacks out, that's all it was, yet many blacks wanted to believe it and they went to California anyway. Did you fall for that story, Leroy?"

"No sir."

"If you never believed in those fabrications, why do you believe the words of that fortune teller?"

"I can't get it out of my head." Leroy put his forearms on the table and clasped his hands together as if he were praying. "I'm so miserable, I'd kill myself, but my death would be the cause of much suffering. I could go on with my days working and surviving, but I don't know when I might be struck dead. There's nothing I can do except wait, and then when I die . . ."

"Yes, yes," I said, interrupting him. "Have you thought about Sabina? She's expecting you to be her husband."

Leroy glanced at the rough, splintery table and looked ashamed. "My death causes her death. I wonder if running far away from here would save her, and everyone else."

"Boy, you'd take the word of a prognosticator over the love of your own woman?"

Leroy looked at me, his eyes huge and filled with melancholy. "I'd stay with Sabina, I would, but not if it ends her life."

It was then I had an idea so radical that I had no doubt that it would shake Leroy from his stupor. Two gifted with the sight had given him similar readings but I held them in such contempt I chalked that up to coincidence. A third with a different prediction (of this I was sure of) would sow the seeds of doubt within him.

I slapped the table. "I want you to come with me and see someone."

"Who's that?"

"Have you been to see Otis Turning about your future?" I asked.

"No," he said.

"Come with me and see Otis," I said.

Leroy's expression held disbelief. "You've never trusted that man. When I lived under your roof and asked if I could work for Otis, you bucked and threatened me with the rod if I ever talked to that man."

"Yes, I did," I said. "There's a reason for everything under the sun. And in this situation, Otis will be of value."

Leroy smiled which gladdened me. "You think he'll give me a completely different future."

"That's my bet," I said. "Might it lift your spirits if a third seer gives you a different story?"

He thought about it, biting at his lower lip. "It might. I'm willing to do something to shake this cloud from me and I need help, which I'm much obliged, Cleve."

"Everything will be fine," I said, my heart warming already at clearing this up.

HE LIVED JUST on the outskirts of town and we walked the well-beaten path carved out by Otis' horse and wagon. Scrub and cactus flanked us, and in the dark I could barely make out those cacti standing like sentries in the pitch black. Coyotes cried out sounding like women in agony far in the desert. The weather was cool and as we got closer to our destination, the gooseflesh covered my forearms.

His clapboard house was well-lit with lantern light in the windows downstairs. His barn stood off to the side of the house with the door shut, but we could hear a horse snuffling.

I gave the door a light rap and the door opened. Otis stood with lantern light washed across half his face—dark, dark skin; high cheekbones and hollowed cheeks as if he were perpetually tasting a sour lemon.

"How may I help you, gentlemen?" he asked, his voice the deepest bass I'd ever heard. He wasn't a big man, being as thin as a whip, but his chest was broad.

I said, "We're wondering if you can help Leroy out here."

He studied Leroy, scrutinizing him from head to toe.

"Leroy Roosevelt, how may I help you?" He asked

and didn't wait for an answer. He stepped back and opened the door wide and said, "Please come in."

Stepping inside his home was like stepping into a different country. First, the smell was pungent and I couldn't place it, but it reminded me of the Chinese settlements in the larger cities of California. Rugs rich with color and tapestry lay on the floor, some with tassels along the edges. The tables, shelves, and writing desk were carved out of oak wood. The furniture was as impressive as the lobby's furniture in the Hotel Beaumont.

I hadn't seen a colored man this wealthy since my early days as an escaped slave. For several weeks I stayed in the home of wealthy black couple on the east coast, in the North. They were part of the underground railroad and even though it's been more than a decade since the end of the War, I still don't feel comfortable about revealing their names.

We sat down at the table. While Leroy's table had been rough, cracked, Otis' table was smooth and polished.

"Water, gentlemen?" he asked. "You must be thirsty."

"I'd be much obliged," Leroy said. He sat across from me.

Otis brought a glass pitcher and crystal glasses

on a metal tray to the table. He poured each of us water and sat down at the head of the table.

He hadn't looked me in the eye since he saw me at the door. Now he regarded Leroy and said, "How may I help you?"

Leroy took a long drink and set his glass on the table. He looked at me. I nodded and he turned to Otis.

"I have a feeling I can't shake," he said. "A feeling that my death is near. I'd like to know my death and how many years I have left."

"Interesting," Otis said and placed his hands flat on the table. He looked at me and said, "And what is your interest in Leroy's future, his death in particular?"

His eyes measured me and he offered such a pleasant smile as he asked the question. I thought of snakes in the grass and I wasn't comfortable under his gaze. It made me remember why I never got close to his wagon when it was in town. This made me consider I wasn't much better than the slaves that believed in the story of that protective root.

I held steady. "I suggested he come here," I said.

"You suggested the visit, yet you and I have never interacted. You've never inquired about my services. You know nothing about me."

"I know your reputation," I said. "You're a prognosticator."

He arched a brow. "If you knew me, you'd know I'm not a prognosticator nor a psychic. I do not 'see' the future, let alone predict it. I'm a necromancer. I speak with the dead and I can tell you only what they tell me."

"How convenient," I said.

Otis scowled at me. "You only measure things with your eyes and if you don't see them, they don't exist. Isn't that right, Mr. Biddle?"

He spoke with the intensity of a preacher and the hair at the back of my neck stood on end. I wouldn't allow myself to feel guilty about using Otis to help Leroy. There's a use for everything under the sun— even Otis—and sometimes a person or thing doesn't have a purpose until an idea strikes.

Otis continued, his eyes unwavering, beating my brow like the slave masters of the South with their whips. "The question," he said, "I have for you: if you don't believe in the things that I do, what motivates you to bring Mr. Roosevelt to my door?"

"I asked him to come along," Leroy said, saving me.

Otis' eyes were still smoldering when he focused on Leroy.

"I do not believe you, Mr. Roosevelt," he said. "But nonetheless I will help you. The dead can tell us many things, but they may not be privy to the circumstances of your death. Ask the question, but I can't guarantee an answer."

He got up and stood behind Leroy with his arms behind his back. Leroy looked at me and sat straight up in his chair. He appeared relaxed, calm.

"I'm going to place my hands on top of your head and communicate with the dead. Do not move or speak. Do you understand?"

"Yes," Leroy said.

Otis looked at me.

"Yes," I said.

Otis lay his hands palms flat, fingers splayed on top of Leroy's head. Both men closed their eyes—Otis with his chin up high, Leroy with his chin lowered as if he were nodding off. Otis' hands did not move. Nobody moved. In the silence, I heard the ticking of a clock somewhere in the house.

Otis turned his head, quickly, side to side. He winced as if he were slapped, once, twice, three times. His breath came fast, his nostrils flaring. I watched him with skepticism. This, I had no doubt, was part of the show.

His eyes opened wide and he stepped back with his hands up as if he were burnt.

Leroy opened his eyes and looked over his shoulder at Otis. "What happened?" he asked.

"I'm sorry to say, Mr. Roosevelt, you won't die an old man, although you won't be young either. Your death will be quite unremarkable, struck down by disease. It will be many years from now."

"A death as unremarkable as my birth," Leroy said. He breathed a sigh of relief.

Otis was lying, holding back something. I just couldn't bite my tongue.

Otis came back around to head of the table and sat down. I said, "What sickness does he die of?"

Otis didn't hesitate. "A fever that will last three days." He looked at Leroy. "You fight it, but it wins in the end."

Leroy looked satisfied. Any death that didn't involve the death of a nation was fine with him.

"Where and when does this happen?" I asked.

Otis looked at me. Twitch at the corner of his eye told me he was irritated with me. "Time is measured differently on the other side. One day in the spirit realm could seem like years to human perception," he said. Then he looked at Leroy. "Many years remain for you. Your heart is still strong."

"Thank you," Leroy said. "How much do I owe you for this?"

Otis held his hand up. "I'm just glad to help, but I'll request you visit my wagon when you see it."

"I'll do that."

I couldn't trust a man—especially one gifted with the sight—who wouldn't ask for something in return for services rendered. This annoyed me. It sat hot and hard inside me.

"Something on your mind?" Otis asked me.

"Kind of you for not asking for something in return," I said, restraining myself from saying more.

"Well gentlemen," he said, standing up. "If we are done here, I must prepare for tomorrow."

The three of us made for the front door. Leroy walked with a light step. The weight he had carried here was gone. Otis opened the door and wished us a good night, and we trudged our way home.

"Feeling better?" I asked him, even though I knew the answer.

"I'm at peace. I needed to hear it from someone like him. Thank you for taking me there."

"None of this would have been necessary if you wouldn't listen to those kind of people in first place," I said.

"I know what you're thinking," he said.

"What's that?" I asked.

"That I'm a fool," he said.

"Better a fool in love, than a fool too scared to move," I said.

THE NEXT MORNING I found Otis outside my home. He sat in his wagon, the horses restless with the stomping of their hooves and flicks of their tails. A fine layer of dust had settled over the wagon, but the red words on the side were still as bright as blood.

"Good morning, Mr. Biddle," Otis shouted. He wore black—a black suit and a wide-brimmed black hat. He looked more suited for a funeral than a business day.

I walked up to his wagon, looked up at him and squinted in the sun when doing so, and said, "What makes you stop here?"

"I need to clarify some things about your friend, Mr. Roosevelt."

"Clarify to him," I said. "Why are you talking to me?"

"There's some things about Mr. Roosevelt you need to hear."

I didn't care what the man had to say, although I

cringed every time he said Mr. Roosevelt. "Call him Leroy," I said.

"Listen now," he said. "Our destinies are inter-twined, the three of us. We make up a trinity, but Leroy alone will judge the future."

"Just what are you selling me?" I yelled.

He continued, "The dead have appointed Leroy the corpse prophet."

"Did you make up this story overnight?" I asked.

But Otis ignored me, and as he spoke he looked off to the distance. "What they told me last night overwhelmed me with its power and I had to be careful in the way I proceeded."

That I knew just by seeing the way Otis had reacted after the reading.

His gaze returned to me. He said, "Leroy will die. Not long from now. I'd say a year, maybe a little more."

The man couldn't see any further into the future than I could. Now he stood before me, heaping stories on lies.

"Upon his death," Otis said, "Leroy will become this 'Corpse Prophet.' We'll know when he's dead by a disturbance across this land that will be hard to ignore."

"Disturbance?" The sun was hot on my face and I was growing restless.

"You and I must reach him when this happens and bring him water. You'll write everything down. Document the experience."

I laughed deep in my chest. I don't know whom the man thought I was, but I was no fool—why would a dead man need water?

I raised my free hand and waved at him. "If you're going to be there, you can document it your own self."

I walked away, leaving Otis and his wagon behind me.

Otis called. "I won't survive!"

I had a mind to get to the Beaumont and he wasn't stopping me. My boot kit grew heavy in one hand, so I switched to the other. His wagon creaked as the tires rolled. The horse brushed past and Otis pulled on the reins.

"It's imperative that you understand our destiny, Mr. Biddle," he said.

I dropped my shoe kit and vaulted up and grabbed the man by his lapels. His expression didn't change—he looked like he had expected anger, as if that was the way to get through to me.

"I'm not buying what you're selling," I said. "Stay clear of me."

"What you believe or don't believe matters not to the dead, let alone to me," he said, his voice harsh in the morning breeze.

I pulled his face closer to mine. "Stay away from me."

I dropped him back in the seat and got down from the wagon. I picked up my kit and was on my way again.

"Your wishes can be respected until the time we're called, Mr. Biddle. That day will be a rude awakening."

I didn't dignify that with a response and kept walking.

If I told Leroy what Otis said, it would undo him once again. Perhaps that's what Otis was after. Get Leroy worked up so that he would need that prognosticator's services. That's why that first visit was free—Otis had bigger plans for us.

I didn't trust Otis and our visiting him had served its purpose. I would not validate Otis's story by telling Leroy about that morning.

❧

LEROY LEFT town within a week as planned, his wagon packed and tied down, covered with canvas. Two horses would pull his wagon across the desert for two days. His rifle lay under the bench. Water jugs hung off the sides like overfilled bladders. He took some wood from his clapboard house hoping it would be of some use in building a home.

He wouldn't be lacking for anything, I thought. Sabina's father was supplying the barn for a shop— the colored citizens of Dobson were in need of a blacksmith. I could argue White Rock was losing one, but honestly it wasn't hard for a colored man in White Rock to receive service at a number of white blacksmiths in town.

The day was cool with the smell of rain that had fallen in the night, which had been welcomed. The sky was light in the east, the sun creeping up over the mountains. Over in the west the sky was a navy blue and stars salting the sky.

Leroy looked good dressed in a good shirt and chaps.

"You should save your good clothes until you arrive in Dobson." I said.

"I have enough good things," he said. "I'll be looking fine for Sabina. Say, bring the extra saddle when you come from for the wedding, now."

"I will," I said. I'd be trekking across the desert with John Washington's family—that's Sabina's relatives-- in a month.

"You know, Cleve," he said, the reins draped over the leather gloves he wore. "Those fortune tellers did something to me."

I frowned. "What's that?"

"We all die, you know? We know we're going to die and what am I going to do, worry about every little fever that comes my way? We make our own destiny, don't you think?"

"You have a whole new life ahead of you," I said, fully believing it with all my heart and soul.

I saw Leroy one more time during the next year in Dobson for the wedding. For the better part of the year I never did meet Otis's eye. His wagon passed by many times, but it took six months before Otis waved at me. I waved back. Sometimes men need to stay away from one another. The hate is no longer stoked, the fire cooled, and we can face each other once again. Until it is cooled, best our paths don't cross.

ON FEBRUARY 5TH, 1877, more than a year after Otis's revelation of prophecy, a preacher stood in front of the Beaumont raising his bible to Heaven, claiming Armageddon had arrived. The reason for this—according to the gossip at the hotel—was because of an upheaval in Dobson.

The morning was cool and comfortable. My dry shirt slid over my skin with the delicacy of a feather. I began the day polishing the boots of two chattering men from Kansas and from them I learned rail service had been disrupted and they were stuck in White Rock.

"I heard the coloreds rioted because of a lynching," said the one with the bushy beard. I looked up at the word coloreds, but neither one took note of me. "And piled the bodies on the railroad tracks. That's why no trains can get through."

The one with the boyish face said, "That sounds more plausible than the preacher's story about a black man's corpse growing fat."

I didn't like hearing about the lynching. Some settlers from the South had taken their sour opinion on former slaves out West. Talk to the wrong person or enter a building through the wrong door, and there might be a Southerner in your face believing you're getting uppity. I wanted to send a telegraph—

or it would have been decent of Leroy to send me one himself to let me know he and Sabina were fine.

Behind me out in the street, hooves clomped through the dirt and wagon wheels creaked as they rolled. A wagon stopped in front of the Beaumont and I kept my head down, focusing on the leather and the silver sheen I was developing upon it.

"Mr. Biddle, it's time!" Otis Turning called.

I closed my eyes. Some part of me believed the gossip coming out of Dobson. Otis simply complicated things.

"Who are you talking to?" one of my customers asked.

"Not you, sir," Otis replied.

I looked over my shoulder. Otis had an expressive brow, all furrowed like neat rows of plowed land. His lips were held in a tight rigid line. "It's imperative that we leave right now, Mr. Biddle. We have a hundred miles to cover."

"You have business with a traveling merchant, bootblack?" The customer asked.

I went back to polishing those boots, the whisking growing to a loud whisper with the speed of my hands. "He thinks I do," I said.

"Mr. Biddle," Otis called again, "you might as

well turn around and talk to me because I am not leaving."

My whole body sagged as if the air had gone out of me. And I shook my head.

"Are we done here, bootblack?"

Truth was their boots were fine and polished. Not that I wanted to be done. I wanted all the distraction I could get.

I touched my brow. "Yessir," I said.

The men stood and fished coins out of their pockets and stepped down from the chairs. As they walked away, I glanced Otis's way and he stared back, waiting. Once the men were down the porch and back into the Beaumont, I stood and made my way down into the street and stood before his wagon looking up at him.

I said, "What makes you think I'm coming with you to—what did you tell me a year ago?—document the events?"

"You're coming with me," Otis said. "Because Leroy is your friend. As for documenting the events, you'll do it, once you see for yourself."

The air smelled like decaying flesh, just a hint of it, which set my nerves on edge. I didn't know it at the time, but that was Leroy over a hundred miles northeast of us.

I gritted my teeth and turned away. "I'm not going with you," I said.

I didn't even make it to the first step back up to the Beaumont Hotel before Otis said, "You'll have fifty dollars if you come along."

This made me turn my head. Otis held fanned U.S. currency. That would be more than a day's work for a day like today with all the business men delayed in town because of the disrupted rail service.

"We can't cover a hundred miles in a day," I said.

"Trust me, Mr. Biddle. We are going to see your friend, Leroy Roosevelt, and we'll be taking the fastest conveyance possible. The fifty dollars is yours for coming along, and there will be fifty more once we get there."

"Fifty now if I come along?"

"For just coming along," he said.

"Because I'm not documenting anything," I said. "I just want to see Leroy." Which was the truth. I still hadn't figured out Otis and his angle, but felt I had the upper hand with my suspicions. It would do my heart good to see Leroy.

Otis patted the bench. The wood sounded sturdy and thick. "The money is yours once you sit up here."

"I'll grab my kit," I said and I ran up the stairs onto the porch and gathered up my rags and tallow. I tucked the case under my arm and carried my squat stool by one leg and went down to Otis's wagon and pulled myself up on the bench seat. Otis held the reins with one hand and got the horses going before I even sat down. With his other hand, he handed me the fifty dollars.

I took his money and with a wide smile he touched the brim of his hat as if to say nice doing business with you. Slipping the money deep into my pocket, I realized what taking his money meant. Leroy was dead. I reflected on Leroy until turbulent emotion welled up inside of me. As if the desert had become cold, an ice chill passed through me.

"If he's dead," I said, "how did he die?"

Otis looked at me as if I were a slow learner. "He was lynched," he said. "As evident of the trains not running and the gossip around town."

My jaw set hard and my fists clenched hard enough I thought my fingers might break. If Otis would have told Leroy the truth, he'd be alive and wouldn't have suffered such a death.

"I know you're angry," Otis said.

I struck my leg with my own fist, the anger

bursting out of me, and for a moment the pain appeased my anger.

"You don't know how angry I am," I said.

I refused to look at him when I spoke. By then he had turned the wagon around in the crowded street, towards the direction of his homestead. Dust clouds rose up and filled the air.

I held my tongue, sulking. I fully believed that we were on our way to see Leroy. Whether we were going to see him alive or dead, I couldn't decide. It left me unsettled and bitter because there was so much gossip about a lynching in Dobson.

I'd believe it when I saw him with my own two eyes.

"You could have saved Leroy by telling him the truth, instead of lying to him about his future," I said, surprised at the spilled words.

We were shouting distance from his homestead. A couple of the older Washington boys and one younger one were milling about in his dooryard. A hot air balloon stood there, too. This struck me as odd, but Otis had always dabbled in things nobody else wished to. I wasn't about to get sidetracked by this man's whims.

"Mr. Biddle," Otis said, "I could say the same of you."

I glared at him.

Otis didn't meet my eye. He stared ahead. "I told you the next morning after Leroy's reading. You had the entire year to give him the story, yet you chose to disregard my words."

I wanted to squeeze his cold heart in my fists and I lunged at him, nearly shoving him off the wagon. His left leg dangled over the edge and his hat sailed off, yet Otis still held the reins.

I gripped him by the front of this shirt as he hollered at the horses.

The balloon loomed overhead when the horses finally stopped, its shadow falling over us as my hands moved to Otis's throat. He bared his teeth in a struggling grimace, and the two Washington boys hopped on board the wagon and pried me away, each hooking around my shoulders and pulling. These boys were young and strong like when Leroy first arrived in town.

"Control yourself, Mr. Biddle," Otis shouted as I found myself pulled off the wagon. I fell backwards and the air rushed out of me as I landed on the two boys. We lay there in the dust, their arms around my arms and shoulders like shackles. I pulled and pulled to sit up, but they gripped me good. Then they each wrapped a leg around one of mine and I was rooted to the ground.

Otis stood up in the wagon, silhouetted against the orange hot air balloon. He leaned on a cane I hadn't noticed before—the cane had the head of a silver eagle. He limped towards the edge of the wagon, looked down at me and shook his head. It occurred to me the man did not look well. He had always been as slim as a reed but now he looked skeletal.

"We don't have time for this, Mr. Biddle. More lives will be lost if we don't do what has been asked of us."

He pulled out a handkerchief and dabbed at his forehead.

"Are you sick?" I asked

"I am dying, Mr. Biddle," he said. "When I told you I would not survive what we are about to do, I wasn't lying. I'd be dead regardless of the prophecy. There's a disease eating away at me just as sure as Leroy is running amok in the northeast."

"Every time you speak, I don't understand a damn word you're saying," I said.

Two other boys helped Otis down from the wagon and he stabbed the ground with his cane.

"Be angry at me," he said. "We both made choices."

"What is Leroy to you? Just a pawn, a mark for some money to be made?"

"Who is he to you?" he asked.

My rage reduced to a trickle, my muscles loosened, tension in my body slipping into the dirt beneath me. Those words he spoke choked me, choked me more than I would have guessed. Who was Leroy to me? He was a friend. More than that. Someone I cared for and educated. He wasn't someone I wanted to see die young.

The only anger I had left was in my face and I sneered at Otis. "He was like a son to me," I said.

He moved closer, his feet stepping tiny steps, the cane taking foot-long leaps. One of the boys tried to help him, but Otis brushed him off with a sinewy wave of the arm. Otis stood at my feet and I probably could have kicked him if I didn't have pity on him and his sickliness.

Otis squatted, one hand holding onto that cane stuck to the ground. "I am dying and I need your help. You and I don't see the world in the same light. Don't you agree?"

"You got that right," I said.

He held out his hand, waiting for me to grab

onto it, but I didn't see how he would pull me up considering the cane he had been favoring.

"Please help me," he said. "Let's go see Leroy." Then he looked at each boy holding me. "Let him go, John," a nod and then a nod at the other one, "Matthew."

The boys scrambled to their feet and I sat up.

I grabbed hold of his outstretched hand. His grip was strong, and as if grace had given him the strength of two men, he bolted upright to stand firm with his own two legs, carrying me with him.

He let go of my hand and another boy, shorter, looked like he was only ten, brought Otis his hat, held it up to the man as if it were the king's crown. "Thank you, Issac," Otis said and lay his hand on the boy's head.

Issac was one of the Butler children, a new family that had settled in White Rock two years earlier.

I looked around and found three of the boys, each stationed at a stake in the ground that surrounded the woven wicker basket underneath the balloon. A stool much like my squat stool (only taller) stood at the base of the basket to aid riders inside. Flames shot up from the burners into the mouth of the balloon.

My stomach flipped at the thought of flight. I've seen hot air balloons used at the county fair in Kentucky, a straight shot up in the sky and back down again, the balloon anchored the whole time.

This ride with Otis would be over a great distance and high the sky with the birds.

Otis slipped on thick gloves—for operating the blast valve, I suspected. He looked at me and said, "Hop in the basket, Mr. Biddle. It's prudent we get flying immediately."

I touched the wicker basket. That too was hot in the morning sun.

Issac ran to my side and looked up at me. "I'll help you inside, sir," he said and offered his hand.

My pride balked at letting a young'n' aid me in the basket, but with the trepidation I was feeling about the ride and more specifically, Dobson. I could use all the help I could get.

I wasn't getting into the balloon for Otis Turning. I was not helping that man. My heart ached with such worry I thought it might burst right out of me. I had to see Leroy and Sabina, just know they were alive. I wouldn't be able to sleep until I heard from Leroy. I'd tolerate a balloon ride.

So I grabbed Issac's hand and he helped me

scramble over the top edge of the basket. Once inside, Otis was right behind me.

The boys handed him his cane and a satchel. At the bottom of the basket were railroad spikes and a hammer to pound them into the ground, and coiled rope. There were three canteens and this reminded me of Otis's claim that our purpose was to bring Leroy water.

"Pull the stakes!" Otis called out. He took his hat off and laid it down inside.

Then he grabbed the blast valve above him and twisted. Fire roared and the ropes running from the balloon to the basket tightened, the fibers rustling as they stretched.

After the stakes were pulled the balloon rushed into the air, too quickly for my taste. My stomach dropped to my feet and I was afraid I had turned green. The boys below us hooted and hollered, waving madly and smiling up at the sky.

Otis waved back, "May your life be blessed with opportunities and the better nature of man," he called to them.

As I was watching the boys slipping away under us, I saw the confusion hit their faces.

"I am sorry to leave all of you," he said, "but my work here is done, so that better futures await you."

The man believed he would die in this ordeal, I realized. Much worse—I was starting to believe Otis and his talk of prophecy. I sank to the bottom of the basket, my back sliding across the rough, woven wicker.

I bent my legs and pulled my knees up, my hip protesting with sharp lance of pain. I laid my head back and closed my eyes.

"You can breathe, Mr. Biddle. We're going up in the sky, not underwater."

I hadn't realized I was holding my breath until he said something. My eyes snapped open, my jaw dropped, and I gulped in some air, my chest aching with each breath.

Otis held one hand on the blast valve.

"Where did you learn to fly?" I asked.

Otis grinned. "I was part of a ground crew for the Union Army and had a preliminary education in hot air ballooning. I didn't personally fly one until after the War, however."

"If man," I said, "had been meant to fly, the Lord would have given him wings."

Sky, pure blue unobstructed sky, lay behind Otis.

"Oh we will conquer the sky," he said. It's a matter of time until we learn to fly in more sophisticated flying machines than this hot air balloon."

"Still doesn't make it right," I said. "It isn't natural."

Otis laughed as he scanned the distance. I had no desire to stand up. I was comfortable where I was.

"Man's curiosity is natural, Mr. Biddle," he said.

"Is that why you're doing this?" I asked. "Huh, curiosity."

"Pardon?"

I laid into him. Yes, my curiosity was as natural as any man's and mine had been piqued by Otis Turning.

"What are you gaining for doing this venture? There's no money to be gained in it—at least I haven't learned of any yet. You never charged Leroy for his reading. And you paid me to come with you. So tell me, Otis, what's in this for you?"

Otis licked his lips. "I'm hoping to see man's better nature prevail."

I grunted. "Man's better nature? There's nothing about his better nature happening here. I've got you lying and according to gossip a colored man has been lynched in Dobson. Otis, man's better nature is as much a figment of your imagination as your prognosticating."

Otis shook his head. He paused and pulled on some cords hanging from above. I had no idea what he was doing but I could feel us float across the sky so I knew we had a good gust of wind. When he finished, he looked at me and said, "You have no hope that man will crawl out of the tar pit of irrational savagery towards reason and enlightenment. I see that in your insular demeanor, your gruff personality, and your unwillingness to look beyond your limited imagination. In fact, Mr. Biddle, I wonder if you have an imagination at all. You have heart, that much I know, for your friend Leroy is like a son to you. However, you have a limited mind and comfortable in the rut you have dug for yourself.

"By the time I breathe my last breath today, I'll see the future of humanity. We'll be more accepting and tolerable; wagers of peace not war; curious and empathetic in our understanding of others and ourselves; virtuous and forgiving. This is humanity's future."

"You should have been a preacher," I said.

Otis had enough imagination for both of us. Eccentric he was, yes, but I wondered if he was plain crazy and here I was in a balloon with him. He had hope for humanity there in the moment. All I had hope for was that I'd see Leroy alive.

We past the time in silence and we rode the wind for a better part of an hour. The smell of decomposing flesh grew stronger, yet I never bothered to raise my head or rise from my place at the bottom of the basket.

"You need to see this, Mr. Biddle," he said after the long silence.

I looked up at him and his face held a grimace, a reflection of whatever he was looking at out ahead of us.

"See what," I said.

A sound like a thousand horses stampeding.

"What is that?" I asked.

"Leroy," Otis said. "Look, I say."

He said Leroy's name with what I thought was disgust. Puzzled, I pulled myself up and looked out at the desert ahead of us.

The dust twirled, rolled, and hung suspended.

Dust washed the northern sky in a grayish brown—the color of ash but with dirt mixed in. The dust mushroomed from its source which I at first thought was a mountain range. This fine, desert dust layered my skin and tickled the inside of my nose. I heard Otis cough. The dust burned my eyes.

Looking beyond the dust, that mountain range changed to a naked colored man lying against the horizon. His feet were bare, pointed straight up, his toes fat, dark drops against the grainy sky. This was a giant man. When I squinted and blinked against the dust, I recognized Leroy's profile. I recognized his sharp nose, square jaw and forehead. Yet even though I recognized him I felt nothing, only numbness. How does one register the impossible?

Dust twirled off of his feet and head into miniature tornadoes, lifting off and carrying debris. Dust rolled along Leroy's arms and legs, rolling like an ocean wave. The stampeding sound had grown louder and it was coming from Leroy. He was growing, plowing through the earth as he grew wider and taller, crushing everything in his path.

This time I coughed and Otis handed me a handkerchief that I accepted mindlessly and crumpled in my fist. I thought of the people in Dobson all crushed under the weight of Leroy's blooming corpse. So much death and more to come if Leroy keeps plowing thorough the desert.

Wind flowed across the basket and the moment would have felt serene except for the dust settling on our skin. The stench was thick up here, however, and I wrinkled my nose as I realized the smell of death and decay had been Leroy all along. In White Rock, it was mild. Above and close to Leroy, the smell had increased tenfold, a pungent odor that summoned bile to my throat.

A thundering boom reverberated through me. Directly below us artillery wagons from the U.S. Army had cannons pointed at Leroy. The black, stubby cannons fired again and explosions detonated over Leroy, sending up more dirt and dust, clouding up the view of Leroy's hand—a hand large enough to swat our hot air balloon.

I grimaced at the cannon fire and the blast against Leroy, but in the end the artillery wasn't having any affect on him. The smoke cleared and his hand was intact and his body continued to roll across the desert.

Through the veil of dust I recognized the men in uniform below were colored, probably the men of the Tenth Cavalry Regiment, posted out here in the desert territory, their equipment and living quarters poorer in quality than any white man's regiment. And the US army saw the colored regiment fit to deal with a colored man's growing corpse.

My heart broke at the sight of Leroy dead in the desert. My mind snapped and I threw my hands to my head and clawed at my hair.

"How?" I said. "Why?" And I even croaked out, "When will it stop?"

Earth couldn't hold his corpse, not even Heaven or Hell, I reckoned.

"Put yourself back together, Mr. Biddle," Otis said with one hand on the burner lever and his focus on Leroy.

My mind was shattering like a mirror because the reality reflected back at me wasn't anything I could make sense of. Here I had become Leroy, who came stumbling distraught out of the Beaumont on a hot summer day worried about what a prognosticator had said to him.

When I looked at Otis, I saw red.

I lunged at him, grabbing the lapels of his shirt. I lifted him off his feet (he weighed no more than a scarecrow stuffed with straw), his hand slipping from the blast valve, and we struck the other side of the basket. Our combined forced caused the basket to rock, threatening to turnover like a boat ready to capsize in the water. His cane—the handle hanging from the edge of the basket—clattered to the floor.

I held him from waist to head over the edge. The ground scrolled out from under us, fluid like a sandy ocean. A covered wagon careened wildly across the desert, crates and cans tumbling out of the back. I leaned into him and I felt our weight teeter over the edge. All I had to do was lean a little more and Otis (or even both of us) would fall.

"We're going to crash into Leroy if you don't let

me go," Otis said, struggling to pry my hands from his lapels.

The ground was much closer than it had been earlier. I turned and saw Leroy's face looming before us. One peculiar sight that remains in my memory: under closed eyelids, Leroy's eyes rolled around. I pulled Otis back up by the lapels and threw him at the flame lever, more out of steaming anger than out of any good sense. Otis regained his footing and steadied himself on the lever. He then adjusted a number of other levers hanging down from the mouth of the balloon.

The sun obscured by the hanging dust shone as a hazy bright orb. The day was no longer bright. Light had dimmed as if life had begun to flee from the world.

The sweep of Leroy's cheek loomed ahead, covered in dust, giving his skin a lighter pallor than in life. I noted Leroy hadn't had a chance to shave before he died. Corkscrew hairs were scattered across his skin. His mouth was open as if to taste whatever the sky offered him. The thought of dirt filling his throat when they buried him whipped its way unwanted into my head.

"Brace yourself!" Otis said.

The folds and curvatures of his ear were covered with dust like the rest of him.

The light in the basket grew dim as we fell into the shadow of Leroy, and the light grew darker still as the balloon above us crumpled and our basket swung onward, deep into Leroy's ear.

Dark as if someone snuffed the candle light.

Like a pail thrown by the handle in underhand fashion, the basket's bottom came up and knocked Otis and I to the back. The balloon filled the opening to Leroy's ear canal, crumpling. As it crumpled, great gusts of hot air flowed over us.

The basket hit the floor of the ear canal. My fingers were pinched between the basket and the floor. The canteens and spikes were strewn about the basket. My head rapped twice against something in the chaos.

Once the balloon deflated, it dropped outside the ear, leaving the opening to the ear canal unobstructed. Dull light painted the walls, floor, ceiling. Light shined off a surface like bone, porous and dry.

The balloon was made of heavy fabric and dropping like a stone. The ropes connecting us to the balloon dragged the basket towards the opening, scraping across the floor like a whisk broom across stone.

Otis scrambled for something in the basket and then he was laying next to me with the floor rolling underneath us. He reached out beyond the basket and with one fist he jammed a spike in the stone floor and with the other hand he swung a hammer, driving down hard on that spike.

The basket's edge jammed against the spike and stopped our slow crawl.

"My God," I said, realizing the size of Leroy's corpse. "How large does he have to be for us to fit inside his ear," I said.

A dark cloud settled over me. I was talking about my friend as if he were an oddity. A friend whom I thought deserved respect.

Otis rummaged around the basket and I heard him strike a match. When I looked up at him I saw him touch a match flame to a wicker of an oil lamp. Orange light washed the gray light coming in from the opening and we could see more clearly inside the basket.

"That survived our landing," I said, referring to the lantern.

"Nothing short of a miracle," Otis said.

He grabbed his cane. He slung one canteen of water over his shoulder and hobbled out of the basket and stepped over the ropes attached to the balloon.

I scrambled on my hands and knees, feeling the rough, gritty floor.

"Water! Otis, how is water going to do Leroy any good?"

I got to my feet and hurried after him.

"First, we find Leroy," he said, his voice echoing off the walls.

I grabbed him by the shoulder and stopped him. He held the lamp between us. Otis was sweating and his right eye drooped. He didn't look well, but in the moment that wasn't my main concern.

"We found Leroy," I said. "We're inside him."

Otis gave me an impatient look.

I stared at him, unable to put the pieces together. All I could see was Leroy swallowing up the desert and that was horrible, but I certainly didn't think I'd talk to Leroy again.

Finally, I spat out, "Is Leroy alive?"

"He'll be alive to you and I," Otis said.

Then I heard Leroy's booming voice coming down the corridor. "Who's down there?" he said.

I had been plunged into the depths of grief at the sight of his corpse and now inside his head my heart swelled at the sound of his voice. Leroy was alive.

My voice shook with joy, "Leroy! Where are you, boy! It's me—Cleve!"

Otis lifted the lamp and stretched his arm further down the canal, shedding feeble light on a doorway. I could just make out the bottom step of what must be a staircase.

"I'm up here. I can't get down!"

There was a distressed note to his voice and I hustled for the doorway. Otis followed, the light growing brighter ahead of me until the stairwell was exposed. The steps were made of the same material as the ear canal. The stairwell spiraled up tightly.

Otis yelled over my shoulder. "He's not alone, Leroy! I'm coming up as well. I'm Otis Turning. You may recall your visit to me a year ago."

"Otis Turning? Well, the company will do me good. Get on up here."

"Are you trapped?" I asked.

"He can't leave," Otis answered.

His answering grated my nerves, but Leroy didn't reply.

Otis touched my shoulder and handed me the lamp. "After you, Mr. Biddle," he said.

I climbed the stairs. Two men couldn't pass each other on that stairwell. Every once in awhile I'd scuff my shoulder or thigh against the rough wall.

The climb sapped my strength and left me breathless with anticipation. The lantern pulled my arm downward as if I held solid steel instead of an item made of brass and glass. Otis's cane step and foot slide lingered behind me. His breathing was harsh and labored. I wondered if the sick man would make it.

I also wondered if the stairs were getting longer as the corpse grew bigger. That would explain why the climb appeared long and never ending. Just as sudden as these thoughts were, I came across a doorway at the top of the stairs and through that doorway standing inside a chamber was my old friend Leroy.

Alive, man alive, Leroy, my old friend, stood with open arms. He looked clean. His face had a vibrant sheen. He wore a crisp white shirt and black slacks, black suspenders.

I reached for him, intending to put my arms around him. That boy wasn't going to get away from me again.

Except he frowned at us and said, "I can't leave this place." Then he dashed through the doorway we had entered.

He came back into the room through a doorway on the other side of the chamber. He appeared there instantaneously. He threw his hands up in the air. "If you two can get in here, why can't I leave?"

Maybe I'd been getting used to impossible things, for it did not surprise me to see Leroy go through one doorway and appear in another.

There was a slab in the center of this chamber. It was taller than your average table.

Above the slab on the ceiling there were two windows that looked like eyes. The windows were very bright—that's how the chamber was washed with light.

Leroy's face crumpled with anger. "They hanged me for talking to a white woman," he said.

Guilt stabbed me deep in my gut.

I said, "Leroy, I knew you would die—not how, but I knew you'd die. The messenger was Otis Turning and I didn't believe him."

"You've never liked those sort of folks," Leroy said. "Of course you wouldn't listen."

"But if I did, you'd still be alive. I'm just as much to blame as Otis. I should have told you."

I trembled. My soul ached over the wonders of that day and the errors and the choices that brought it. Leroy had no reason to forgive me.

"Hush, old man," he said. He glared at me. I could see the anger underneath his skin, coursing though his blood. It was the tightness in his jaw and that tremble in his temple. "What's done is done and you'll have to live with it."

My heart sank at the same time a burden was lifted off my shoulders. I was wounded that he was angry with me—on another day I might have laughed because it was as if our roles had been reversed: now he was schooling me.

As I stood there with a sense of helplessness and sadness, Leroy's cane and feet scraped across the rough floor.

"Allow me to explain, Mr. Roosevelt. Your corpse —due to your wrongful death—is growing. You're already as big as a mountain. We're inside your head right now."

"My death wasn't suppose to wreak havoc," Leroy said.

"It's swallowing the desert," I said. "I didn't believe it until I saw it. Crushed Dobson."

"My God!" Leroy said. "What about Sabina?"

I had no answer.

Otis reached out his cane and tapped the slab.

"Mr. Roosevelt, have you been seeing the future?" he asked.

"Every time I touch that thing," Leroy said.

"And how do you judge the future?"

Leroy looked perplexed. "There are things I don't understand. There are horrors but amazing things too."

"Are you a prognosticator now?" I asked Leroy.

"I guess I am whenever I touch that slab."

I pointed at Otis, my hand shaking, and said, "That's what you wanted. You didn't care about Leroy. You just wanted to see your better future."

Otis pulled the canteen from his shoulder. "And to bring your friend water."

"I'm not thirsty," Leroy said.

"Mr. Roosevelt, water will end the monstrosity of your corpse."

Otis lifted the canteen by the strap. I wasn't convinced stopping the corpse would bring Leroy any justice.

I curled my fingers, ready to grab Otis, and stepped in his direction. He bounced his cane on the floor and it slipped farther up his hand. Then he swung it at me as I approached, the silver eagle's head connecting with my jaw. An explosion of blood rushed into my mouth, the pain burned, I saw stars. My head snapped to the right, and my body followed. I plummeted to the floor.

"You've attacked me twice so far today, Mr. Biddle. There will not be a third."

I waited for the world to stop spinning and I spat out blood. Red, red, blood red is all I saw in my head. Part of it was the white hot pain, otherwise it was good old anger stoked at Otis.

"I have a good mind to break that cane over your head," Leroy said. "Step away from him."

Leroy came to me while Otis stepped back, the tip of his cane back on the floor.

"Mr. Roosevelt, if the future is fine by your judgment, better it should end now."

I pushed myself up from the floor and remained on my hands and knees.

"Why must it all be up to me?" Leroy said.

"The circumstances of your death. You died of bigotry and hatred," Otis said.

Leroy pulled, hauling me up by my shoulders. I got my feet under me, swayed a bit, but I held steady.

"Let it all end, Leroy. Grow big enough to crack through the earth," I said.

"But Sabina and my child," he complained.

"Child?" I pushed away from him and staggered.

He gave me a sad smile. "I didn't have the chance to send you a letter before all this," he said. "We're expecting a child, Cleve. I was going to be a father."

I didn't have the heart to suggest Sabina and the

child might be dead already. "Is the future so bright that you'd let your child grow up in it?"

Leroy looked at me in a sad, almost impatient way. "People will persevere. It's that clear to me."

If I could give him my anger—which lay thick and murky in my heart—I would. "You forgive them for hanging you?" I asked.

He knocked his head back as if I had swung at him. "Me wanting the devastation to stop isn't the same as forgiving the men who hanged me, and all the people who stood around and watched," he said.

Anger tightened his face and angry tears welled in his eyes—I could see it in the light permeating the chamber.

He said, "They were wearing masks of unquestioning inhumanity. And I wasn't a human being to any of them. Nobody questioned the charge of attempted rape. They watched me die as if I were some side show. My humanity was stripped away in that moment. I want my humanity back. That's why I want this," he said waving his hand around the chamber, implying his burgeoning corpse, "to end. It's enough devastation."

He shook his finger at me. "Don't tell me my family might be dead. Promise me you'll go out and find them and tell them that I love them.

That's all I ask of you. The future looks bright enough as long as my child has a life to live. Obstacles may be stacked up against him, but there will always be people who love him and take care of him."

The cold, thick hatred that had coated my heart melted away and I admired his optimism, his uncompromising hope in a white man's world that his own child would prevail. His love for his own child eclipsed the bigotry.

"Promise me you'll find Sabina," he said.

"I will," I said, the words tumbling out without even thinking of them. My whole heart was in those words.

"May I, Mr. Roosevelt?" Otis asked as he waved his arm at the slab and the windows on the ceiling.

"You don't need to ask my permission," Leroy said.

"I thank you just the same," Otis said. He looked as joyful as a child in a candy store.

Otis touched the slab and the light from the windows flared, brightening the chamber, so bright the light pierced my skull and sliced my mind. I closed my eyes and clutched my head, but the pain held on and on, until . . .

It was gone. I opened my eyes and saw Otis with

a considering look on his face as if he had felt no pain at all.

"What a future indeed," he said. He held the canteen out for Leroy. "Drink this and your soul will be at rest."

"Much obliged," Leroy said. Then he looked at me.

"You were like a son to me," I said.

He smiled. "I know," he said.

He took his drink. The moment the water touched his tongue he grew transparent and liquefied and splashed down. The canteen clattered to the floor.

I had no time to react before the floor turned transparent and liquefied.

Our legs sank into water and a wave crashed upon us. Water rushed into my ears. The chamber was gone, Leroy irrevocably turned completely to water. I had no time to mourn for I had to fight for survival.

The water struck me with such force I spun and tumbled. I didn't know which way was up. A current pulled at me like a river. Otis flowed past with his cane twirling along behind him.

My jaw stopped aching in the tumult. The water was warm. My lungs burned for air.

My head broke the surface, water pouring down my face as I gasped for breath. The sky still possessed the copper dust haze, the sun obscured— a bright orb behind that curtain of dust.

My head went under. I tread water and broke the surface again. I was floating on top of a huge wave with water sloping down on all sides of me with more water below, stretching out in all directions. The desert was out there—I just couldn't see it. I didn't have time to look. The wave shot me down- ward as if I rode a rug shaken out, riding the undula- tions as it snapped in the air.

Fast, like a mountain river building up speed. I was helpless. All I could do was keep my head above the surface. The water was as blue as the sky.

My heart pounded in my ears at the speed I was being carried, like the rushing rapids sure to smash me against rocks in an unexpected place. I lifted my face and the wind carried the dripping water off my skin.

The air shimmered in the distance. Cactus and mesquite trees shot into the air.

The wave smoothed out—I was almost level with the ground. I spotted boards and barrels bobbing in the water. Caught sight of a couple bodies floating, too, and my heart sank for Leroy. He wouldn't care for the deaths.

Water churned to mud, cutting around cactus and rock. Sagebrush was lifted out of the ground and carried by the current. My legs struck ground and I tumbled forward, my feet and hands sinking into soft mud. My head went under. Mud brown water filled my throat and I gagged. I lifted my head above the surface streaming past me and vomited the muddy water from my throat. It was thick and gritty and the feeling remained in my throat and on my tongue.

Bodies and debris struck my backside and I fell forward, my head underwater again. When I surfaced another wave came at me. On this wave I saw a dead horse, more wood and debris.

I scrambled up to run away from the incoming wave but my feet sank, pulling me down into the muck. The sound of the approaching wave sounded like the ocean to me. A whispered roar that spoke of undercurrents and things I could not fathom. I ran, although it was like running through molasses.

The water flowed around me with such force it nearly knocked my legs out from under me. Off in the distance I saw two of the soldiers sitting on their horses. I think they saw me, for they didn't hesitate to ride into the oncoming water, the horses' hooves throwing up mud and water. They were at least a mile away and it would take time to get to me with all the water and debris.

I fell forward into the mud, a wave smashing over my back. When I staggered up again, more bodies and debris floated around me. There he was: Otis, floating by on his back with arms outstretched.

He was dead and I knew it, for he had foretold it. The water level lowered to my ankles and Otis settled down into the muck. Determination ignited inside of me. I didn't want to be the sole bearer of what had happened that day, so I lifted my feet out of the muck, and ran to Otis.

My breath ragged in my chest, I hooked my hands underneath his arms and pulled him to a barrel that was partially submerged in the muck. Don't ask me where I got the strength, but I lifted and threw him face forward over the barrel. I needed to get the water out of him. I lifted his feet and pushed with all my might to roll him.

"You're not going to die on me, Otis," I said. "You're going to be wrong about one thing, you prognosticating bastard!"

His clothes were soggy and dripping. My strength sapped away, I dropped his legs and stumbled onto my knees against the barrel and I pounded my fists against his back. Water splattered from his wet shirt.

I pulled him down and he landed in the muck with a splat. Then I pounded his chest until I was surprised by the eruption of muddy brown water from his mouth. He coughed and coughed, his whole body shaking. His eyes were closed but he was breathing.

"God damn you, Otis!" I said.

He peered at me, his eyes wide and vibrant. "Mr. Biddle," he said. "Have you seen the road up ahead? I know you can."

I stared at him. That man had rarely made sense to me.

"Can you see it?" he said. "November 2nd, 2008."

"Hey!" a booming voice came from behind. I turned and saw the two soldiers running through the muck, coming for us. Their horses were left behind in shallower water. They ran splashing through mud. The yellow bandannas were wet, wrapped around their necks, and plastered against the front of their uniforms. The bandannas were filthy with brown dust.

"Hey, old man," one of them called. "Is your friend alright?"

When I looked at Otis he had the look of a dead man, his eyes wide and unblinking, staring at the incredible distance between here and the heavens.

I CUPPED my hands under the flow of water from the pump. The water was cool, overflowing my hands and splattering in the dust. I slurped the water. It tasted crisp and clean. This water was the man whose corpse filled a desert. Like drinking the blood of Jesus Christ, I was drinking the water of Leroy Roosevelt. My friend, my son.

An oasis in the desert had become Leroy's legacy. You see, the water that had been his giant body remained on the surface for awhile. At least until it settled in fissures and crevices underground and created springs.

Although Dobson had been demolished, it was being rebuilt.

I pumped the handle again and more water poured from the spout. As I drank greedily—as if Leroy himself could sustain me—walls and frames of buildings were being erected all around me. Hammers pounding nails came from all directions like dogs barking in the streets.

In six months, Dobson had grown back to half its former size. Wagons filled with supplies and workers constantly coming and going. Dust filled the air with every pass of a wagon. Falling dust never failed to remind me of the sight of Leroy's burgeoning corpse in the desert.

I paused and allowed a Chinese boy to fill his bucket and go scampering to his father and other workers on the new saloon going up behind me. At that pump I drank and watched the march of progress.

I had visited Sabina and looked into the eyes of Leroy's son. She settled here near the springs. "It just seems right," she said to me. "The water makes me think of Leroy. He will always be with us."

She named Leroy's son, Cleve, after me. "Because Leroy had been fixing to name his son that before any of this happened," she said.

The bittersweet gesture invoked tears and I'm not usually a crying man, especially not in front of a woman.

Little Cleve is a big boy, just like his father. Large brown eyes that could swallow you and the world whole. Big hands, large feet, and heavy for a one year old.

I had plans on settling in Dobson myself and I

was in town hoping to purchase a plot of land. I was standing at that pump when Mary Wilson found me.

"Excuse me, Mr. Biddle?" she said.

She stood a good ten feet away, standing half turned, staring at the roofers on top of a new hotel. Her dress and hoop skirt were pale blue, but her bonnet was as deep blue as the sky. Her hair was tucked away under her bonnet. Her face looked weathered from the wind and the sun.

She glanced at me and looked away five or six times. There were plenty of men (white and colored) around hauling wood and swinging hammers. Plenty of women meandering down the streets with lunch pails and carrying water. However, nobody was looking at us. Through the cacophony of the bustling town, we were the only two people in the world. And she was worried somebody might see her talking to a colored man.

"Are you talking to me?" I asked.

"Forgive me, I'm Mary Wilson and I teach school here in town. I noticed you were with Sabina leaving the feed store earlier today and she had said you'd be in town." She made an act of looking down the street and touching her face in thought.

"You know Sabina?" I asked.

"Yes, I do. She told me you were Leroy's pa."

"That's right, I am."

She closed her eyes tight and muttered to herself, a prayer perhaps. When she opened them she said, "I'm sorry, Mr. Biddle, but I'm the reason why Leroy was killed."

I sputtered with laughter.

"You're guilty only if you're the one who put the noose around his neck," I said.

She grimaced at the word noose. "I'm the one who talked to him, Mr. Biddle. I'm the one who initiated the conversation. I was interested in his life experience. I got him in trouble when all I wanted to do was make a friend."

It dawned on me why she was acting peculiar. She wasn't afraid to look a colored man in the eye. No, she'd have no shame in that if the circumstances were different. She was afraid what white men might think if they saw another colored man talking to her.

For a moment anger tensed my muscles and the set of my jaw. I thought: how could this woman be so careless? She talked to one colored man and he got lynched—what made her think it wouldn't happen to me?

"I wish not to get you in trouble," she said, glancing at me once with a gentle, hesitant smile.

The hammering ceased and the foreman at the

hotel barked orders at the men on top of the roof. A stage passed by and I felt the pounding hooves under my feet.

A year had passed since Leroy died—you'd think I'd be beyond that kind of anger. Mary Wilson surprised me. Not to mention the truly guilty ones had already died—Deputy Thomas and the Johnson brothers died in the early hours after Leroy's murder. How's that for poetic justice—they had murdered him and his corpse crushed them.

"People have come up with tall tales to explain what happened here," she said. "Most people would rather forget and pretend it was some natural disaster."

"And not some horrid lynching," I added.

She flinched at that, too. Then she carried on, "I'm sorry for your loss. Will you forgive me? For the part I played in it?"

She looked visibly shook—tears streaked down her cheeks, catching glimmer of sunlight. She looked at the dust at her feet.

Here was a woman burdened by guilt with no one to help her lift it. Who would?

Mary Wilson touched my heart in that moment. A burden upon my shoulders had been lifted and I felt at ease for there was a white woman who saw the clear and indisputable bigotry and hatred perpetrated by other whites.

"Look at me," I said.

She wrung her hands hard enough and with such ferocity, I thought she might wring blood from them.

"Look at me," I said again.

She raised her chin and turned her head. Her eyes looked green from where I stood.

"It's not your fault Leroy died," I said. "But if it makes you feel any better, Ms. Wilson, I forgive you. Now dry those eyes."

She took in a giant heave and shuddered with a sob that had a hint of a grateful guffaw. Then she wiped at her tears.

"Thank you, Mr. Biddle," she said.

Now her gaze held steady on me. Neither one of us were concerned about the men working on the buildings. As if the shackles were thrown down, we were free, in the moment, just the two of us. For the rest of America it will take a little more time.

Let me explain.

It must have been that bright light inside of Leroy's head. Now, on many mornings, I awake with a new image of America's future. I know these images are from the future because the dreams are vivid and detailed. Sometimes I see dates.

Otis had been an optimistic man who heard the dead telling him the future. He wanted to "see" the future, both with his head and his heart, but all he'd been able to grasp were words from the dead floating in the ether we the living could not see. That is until he looked into those windows inside Leroy's head.

Now I have become more than the man I despised. I see things. I see them clearly in my dreams.

Leroy's corpse will hang over America for many years. I'm being metaphoric here—and I find this odd since I'm essentially a literal man. Leroy represents the Negro. The Colored. The Black Man. While we gained ground with the Emancipation Proclamation there would be challenges and violence up ahead.

Black Laws and segregation will rein on. Up ahead I have seen a preacher named Martin Luther King fighting for the Civil Rights Law and will be assassinated while doing so. This law will come to pass over eighty years from now. Hardly a bright and shining future from my point of view.

Yet forty some short years from there, the nation

elects a man named Barack Obama as the first black president of the United States. November 2nd, 2008. The same date as Otis's last words spoken to me.

That's what he saw in those bright windows inside Leroy's head. Something will shift in the conscience of American society for a black man is elected president. My heart gladdens at the thought, at the acceptance and trust, but is this evidence—by Otis's words—of our better natures?

The future still holds bigotry and hatred, flames that will burn brightly throughout the majority of the next century. Change is never easy. Even when coming to terms with our better natures.

As I looked at Mary Wilson I thought of one of those many dreams: the suffrage movement in the next century would bring voting rights to women. In fact, the same year the first black man is elected president a woman will be in the same race for the White House. This is the nation's future: equality and freedom for man or woman of any race or creed to reach their potential.

"I have one more thing to ask of you, if you don't mind," she said. "I hate to take up more of your time."

"What is it, Ms. Wilson?"

"Will you tell me about Leroy Roosevelt? You can

send a letter to the schoolhouse. If addressed to me, I'll receive it."

I stared at her, which she took as hesitation on my part and she began wringing her hands again.

"I just want to know him. I mean, really, Mr. Biddle," she said, shaking her head. "It would be the same if he had died in a stampede or drowned or got deathly ill. It's his humanity I want to know about, which his race is just one part."

I'll tell her about Leroy. He was a married man, an expectant father. He liked working with horses and could swing a hammer down on the anvil quick and powerful. I'll tell her and treat her with the dignity she deserves.

You see, my dreams are simply visions of the future. I cannot touch them and they cannot touch me. Will they come to pass? Moments like the one with Ms. Wilson where we converse and listen to one another make me think our better natures will prevail. It's the only way I can get myself to believe.

The End

ABOUT ROB VAGLE

Rob Vagle has been writing short fiction for over thirty years with stories in Realms Of Fantasy, Strange New Worlds, Heliotrope, Fiction River, Pulphouse, and more.

You can sign up for his newsletter, Dispatches From This Side Of Wonder, at www.robvagle.com

facebook.com/robvagle
bsky.app/profile/robvagle
instagram.com/robvagle
threads.com/@robvagle

ALSO BY ROB VAGLE